Captain Bumble
a play

Captain
Bumble
First
Mate
Cookie
One-Eye
Jake

First Mate:

Captain Bumble, Captain Bumble,
you're wanted on the deck.

Captain:

Go away, First Mate.
I'm having my dinner.

First Mate:

But, Captain, a pirate ship is coming.
It's One-Eye Jake and his men.

Captain:

One-Eye Jake? Blood and thunder! What a cheek! I'll blow his ship right out of the water – as soon as I've eaten my dinner.

First Mate:

Aye, aye, sir.

Captain:

Cookie! I'd like another pot of soup.

Cookie:

But you've just had a pot of soup – *and* chicken – *and* pudding.

Captain:

I'm hungry. And I can't fight when I'm hungry.

Cookie:

Oh, all right. Here's one more pot of soup.

First Mate:

Captain Bumble,
Captain Bumble,
you're wanted
on the deck.

Captain:

What is it this time?

First Mate:

It's the pirates.
One-Eye Jake and his men.
They're climbing up the side
of our ship.

Captain:

Climbing up the side?
Blood and thunder! What a cheek!
I'll get that Jake. I'll cut off his head –
when I've had my dinner.

First Mate:

Aye, aye, sir.

Captain:

Cookie, get me
some more chicken.

Cookie:

Did you say
more chicken?

Captain:

I did.

Cookie:

All I do is cook, cook, cook. Oh, all right. Here's some more chicken.

Captain:

Good. I can never fight when I'm hungry.

First Mate:

Captain Bumble,
Captain Bumble,
you're wanted on the deck.
Please come.

Captain:

I'm still eating my dinner.

First Mate:

One-Eye Jake has
tied up all your men.
Now he's got your
treasure.

Captain:

My treasure?
Blood and thunder!
What a cheek!
I'll throw him
to the sharks.
That's what I'll do –
after I've had
my dinner.

First Mate:

Aye, aye, sir.

Captain:

Now let me see. I think I'll have another helping of pudding. Cookie! More pudding, please.

Cookie:

What? More pudding as well?

Captain:

I'm still hungry.

Cookie:

But you've been eating all day. And I've been cooking all day. Oh, all right. Here's some more pudding.

One-Eye Jake:
Ah-ha!
So there you are,
Captain Bumble.

Captain:
One-Eye Jake!
What are you
doing down here?

One-Eye Jake:
You wouldn't come up
on deck, so I've come
down here to fight.

Captain:

I'll fight you, Jake. And I'll beat you.
But first I'll have my dinner.

One-Eye Jake:

What's that you're eating? Pudding?
My cook never makes me pudding.
Give me a bite.

Captain:

No.

One-Eye Jake:

Just one bite.

Captain:

Not one.

One-Eye Jake:
Please. I'll let go all your men.

Captain:
No.

One-Eye Jake:
I'll give you back your treasure. Look – I'll give you some of my treasure as well. And you'll never see me again.

Captain:
Oh well – just one bite.

One-Eye Jake:
Mmmm. Yum, yum, yum.

Captain:

Now go away, Jake.
And don't come back.
Good. He's gone.
Cookie! Are you there, Cookie?

Cookie:

Yes, Captain Bumble?

Captain:

I'm hungry again.
Get me a big
chocolate cake.

Cookie:

Oh, no!
That's the end.
All you do is eat,
eat, eat. I've *had* you
and your eating.

Cookie goes out and comes back with bag.

Captain:

Hey! Where are you going, Cookie?

Cookie:

To cook for One-Eye Jake.
I'll be a pirate cook.

Captain:

But you *can't.*
What will I do without you?

Cookie:

You can eat mouldy old bread.
There's plenty of that.
Goodbye, Captain Bumble.

Captain:

Come back, Cookie, come back!
Blood and thunder! What a cheek!
He's gone to cook for that no-good Jake.
Oh well – I'll have to eat
this mouldy old bread.